...who now is a member
of the HORRIBLE HARRIET
fan club.
H. Harriet: President.

HORRIBLE HARRIET'S
INHERITANCE

In her own words

ASSISTED BY
Leigh HOBBS

ALLEN&UNWIN
SYDNEY · MELBOURNE · AUCKLAND · LONDON

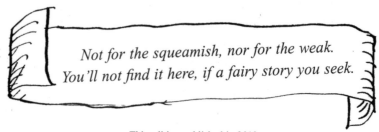

Not for the squeamish, nor for the weak.
You'll not find it here, if a fairy story you seek.

This edition published in 2012

Copyright © Leigh Hobbs 2012

Allen & Unwin
83 Alexander Street
Crows Nest NSW 2065
Australia
Phone: (61 2) 8425 0100
Fax: (61 2) 9906 2218
Email: info@allenandunwin.com
Web: www.allenandunwin.com

A Cataloguing-in-Publication entry is available from the National Library of Australia
www.trove.nla.gov.au

ISBN 978 1 74114 985 2

Cover design by Leigh Hobbs and Sandra Nobes
Text design by Sandra Nobes
Set in 14 pt Times New Roman by Sandra Nobes
This book was printed in October 2012 at McPherson's Printing Group,
76 Nelson St, Maryborough, Victoria 3465, Australia.
www.mcphersonsprinting.com.au

4 6 8 10 9 7 5 3

MIX
Paper from
responsible sources
FSC
www.fsc.org
FSC® C001695

The paper in this book is FSC® certified.
FSC® promotes environmentally responsible,
socially beneficial and economically viable
management of the world's forests.

Miss Horrible Harriet wishes to thank Erica Wagner, Elise (Eagle Eye) Jones
and Sandra Nobes for their wonderful help with this book.
Mr Leigh Hobbs was just a nuisance.

CONTENTS

Look...

Here I am composing some of my
beautiful poems using the ancient method.
That is, pencil applied to paper with my thoughts added

Photo OF L. HOBBS.
IMPROVEMENTS by me
H. HARRIET

A WORD OF WARNING!
from Mr Leigh Hobbs

Quickly, while there's time! This may be my only chance to speak to you, the unfortunate people who've picked up this book... I assume by accident.

Seeing that you have, I advise you not to proceed beyond this page, for if you do you will enter a worrying world, a disturbing place – that is, the frightening mind of Miss Horrible Harriet.

Until now, she has been a very private person, comfortable on her nest in the roof of her school, busy keeping an eye on the teachers doing her homework in the cellar.

But following a life-changing event, presented here in the book you are holding, Miss Horrible Harriet's world is about to be revealed.

Oh no! I hear a noise – H.H. approaches...

You have been warned. Continue at your peril.

Leigh HOBBS.

(ASSISTANT TO MISS H.H.)

Here's me taking a well-earned break from diary-writing and ~~poetry~~
← poetry.

INTRODUCTION
by
Miss Horrible Harriet

Dear Readers,

You are the lucky ones, and don't forget it. For you are about to learn all about me (well, a lot – not everything, because some things must stay secret). Don't expect rubbish like beauty tips or manners advice (yuk!) in this book, because I'm not interested in that stuff, and I'm the boss of what's between the covers.

What you will find is much more interesting. In fact, dare I say it (yes, I do), it's thrilling, and it's this: Something exciting happened to me not so long ago. I'm going to tell you about it. And for your added enjoyment – because I want you to think you've got your money's worth (unless this book is stolen... if it is, OWN UP!) – along the way I've also included some extra and exciting things about me. For example, pictures and photos of me doing things at home, a few of my brilliant poems, plus a few exciting recipes etc etc. All of which I ORDER YOU TO KEEP SECRET! This is just between me and you.

No PEEKING without permission!
by order of ME.
(H.H.)

On reading this book you will straight away become a member of the exclusive H. HARRIET FAN CLUB. (More details in the back.) You will also enter my brain, and never be the same.

Lucky H. Harriet, having her own book! I can hear you thinking. Well, just how many of YOU have had the truly amazing things happen to you that happened to me…the things you are about to learn about? And by the way, ignore the advice of that awful and nosy Mr Leigh Hobbs. He is but my lowly assistant.

Read on! By Order.

Yours Truly,

Horrible Harriet

x xx

Just try, teachers everywhere,
to make me a good girl,
if you dare.
Read my motto if you're smart,
the scary words I wrote by heart.
Harriet be bad, Harriet be brave,
never be nice and never behave!

GOOD GIRL

what are you looking at?!

Chapter 1

MY WONDROUS SURPRISE

It was the school holidays and no one was about. Well, I was here, of course, up in my room writing a brilliant poem. Suddenly my concentration was rudely ruined by a loud banging noise. It was coming from the front door. I flew downstairs in a great hurry. When I opened the door I saw a very strange sight.

There, kneeling on the mat, was Fred the postman. 'Your Majesty!' Fred said. He was sort of smiling, and his eyes were wet with tears. Naturally I was surprised, for most days, after flinging my mail over the front fence, Fred fled. But today, he pushed a big envelope into my hand. It was addressed in fancy writing to 'Her Royal Highness, Miss Horrible Harriet'.

My fingers fumbled as I gently opened the precious envelope. I began to read (a skill taught to me by Mr Boggle, my teacher, whose glasses are very thick)…

The Palace

Tuesday

Dear Miss Horrible Harriet,

It is with great pleasure that I write to inform you of a recent discovery which leads us to believe that you are a long-lost member of the Royal Family.

If you would be so kind as to add the names of any royal ancestors you can recall to the empty spaces on the enclosed chart showing your family tree, thereby proving your links with the Royal Family, you will be able to claim your royal inheritance. This, by the way, includes a castle – more a stately home actually – on the coast.

I trust this finds you well, and that you will supply the information required as soon as possible.

You shall in the meantime be addressed as 'Your Royal Highness'.

Yours Truly,

Sir Ponsonby Flashback

Ponsonby F

Royal Secretary

P.S. There is a slight chance you may even be a queen.

A shiver shot down my spine. I knew nothing would ever be the same again – for Fred, either. This turned out to be true, as I decided to knight him on the spot.

'Arise, Sir Fred,' I said. It was the least I could do. He was grateful for it, and rightly so. I stood stunned, staring at Sir Fred, who was still startled by his recent knighting.

Quickly I calmed down. Now that I was a V.I.P. I needed to take control and give orders. I waved my arm. 'Be gone, Sir Fred,' I said. 'I have royal business to attend to.'

'Yes, Your Majesty,' said Sir Fred as he humbly backed away from my royal presence, down the path and out the school gate.

'ARISE, SIR FRED,' I said.

I studied closely the contents of the envelope.
Also included were some keys. 'Use only for stately
home,' said the attached instructions. I held aloft the
chart with my family tree on it. *This shouldn't be TOO
much of a problem*, I thought, looking at the gaps that
needed filling.

Even though it wasn't definitely decided that I
would end up a queen, I could tell Sir Pooncenbury
Splashback was hinting it would be so. I made a note
to look up the word 'inheritance'.

I began training for my new royal life straight away. It was much more fun than homework, not that I ever had to do any – I left that to Miss Plume and Mr Scruffy in the cellar. I improved my vocabulary greatly, too, so that I would be able to speak nicely when launching a ship or opening parliament. After nearly an hour of mouth exercises and serious concentration, I sounded quite royal.

As Queen I would surely be pestered to sign autographs and all sorts of other things, so next I practised getting my signature right. After that I was exhausted and decided to retire.

My day is done; I'm off to bed.
I'm on my nest; it's time to rest.
I cannot sleep, although it's night,
till in my diary I do write
this day's events —
what's come and been.
Tomorrow H.H. may be queen!

Chapter 2

MY HAPPY CHILDHOOD
in words and pictures

Here is a rare glimpse of my soft side.
← Do not mistake this for WEAKNESS.
H. H.

TOP STUDENT
HORRIBLE HARRIET

I was keen to move into the palace as soon as possible, so I decided to look for clues immediately. My photo album was the obvious place to start. Here are some of the photos to share with you, lucky Reader...

↑ As you can see I was a beautiful baby. Here I am with my dolly Deidre, and this is me with my first big ~~fangs~~ teeth

↓

MOST DIFFERENT BABY AWARDED TO H. HARRIET

I spent many happy days in my playpen. They put a roof on it just for me.

Sometimes I was taken for a walk. But I liked to relax in my pram and greet admirers more.

18

I shared many fun times with sweet Freda, my pet RAT.

↑ Here's me with my pet pug, Princess.
And this is Betty the Bitser ↓

A kiss for princess so she doesn't get jealous. (of Freda)

Here I am at my fifth birthday party ←

Here I am on my first day of school. I thought fun times had ended forever.

This is my teacher, mr Boggle. He can't see very well →

22

Here's my ID card.
I learnt to sign
my name on the
first day of school.

→

Student photo

Student name

Horrible Harriet

I had lots of fun times at school
after all. Look, here I am playing
jump the foot.

ACTRESS OF THE YEAR H.HARRIET

It wasn't long before my talents were discovered. Here I am starring in the school musical. I was Fenella the Fairy.

24

↑ I make friends
quickly.
This was
rest time.

Here I am
ready for
anything!
→

STUDENT REPORT CARD

Student Name .....Horrible Harriet....

Behaviour .....Excellent!....

Attitude .....Always ~~good~~ perfect.... EXCELL-ENT.

Attendance .....At school every day....

Punctuality .....On time all the time....

Homework .....ALWAYS IN on time....

Subjects

MATHS .....A TOP student! 100/100....

ART .....A GENIUS   99/100....

SCIENCE .....Brainy   98/100....

SPORT .....The Champion at everything. 95/100....

MANNERS .....Perfect   100/100....

General Comments .....miss Harriet is a helpful and very talented student for whom I predict a great FUTURE....

Class teacher .....Mr Basil Boggle....

As you can see, I got an excellent report. I kindly helped Mr Boggle write it, as he lost his glasses that day.

↑ These are both of my best friend, Babs.
She loves my home-cooked lunches ↓

I ~~was~~ am good
at everything
at school.
Here's me in
dancing class

Best Ballerina
~~Rosemary Brook~~
HORRIBLE
HARRIET

I am also a composer. Here I am playing my first concerto →

↑ I sometimes use my ballerina skills in basketball. No wonder my report said I was a champion.

This is me on dress-up day. "You are a great actress already," says MR Boggle.

Happy days with my school friends.

Well, that was all very interesting, I'm sure you are thinking, and of course everything is of interest in this book. But alas none of these thrilling photos helped me in my search for ancient relatives. What would I say to Sir Ponsippy Flashlight?

I was feeling very sorry for myself when suddenly I saw a photo that reminded me of a special trip I once went on, and something came into my head.

Before I can show it to you, however, I must speak in hushed tones of a little secret.

Now, many of you will have heard of Mr Chicken. I know you will complain if I don't do this, so I am going to mention him in this book. You will see him a bit, but not too much – too much of him is not a good thing, for he can be a pest. (He certainly eats a lot. My fridge is always empty after his visits. Did you know he likes to eat sandwiches by the hundred!!!)

You see, he has his own book, all about his trip to Paris, where I wasn't invited, so I am not going to let him star in this book, do you understand? This is MY book, and I won't be letting him take your attention away from me! So I have ordered that he be in disguise as much as possible.

Don't bother to write and ask why he appears and disappears in my book, because I'm not interested in explaining. Mr Chicken and me are friends for sure, but I have to keep him under control. Or else there will be trouble, and maybe even some tears.

My Secret Friend, by H. Harriet
Some nights when I'm wide awake
I write a poem or bake a cake,
or better still I phone my friend,
who'll meet me before moonlight's end.

Chapter 3

MUSEUM DISCOVERIES

Now that you know the secret (of my friend Mr C.), here is the photo I mentioned before of a special trip – the clue I'd been looking for. The memories came back as if it were yesterday. (In fact, it had actually been the week before.) My class had gone with Mr Boggle to the museum. Looking back, I realised that was the first time I'd ever felt royal – so perhaps it could help me now in my thrilling quest to fill out my family tree…

↑ This is me arriving at the museum.

I was glad to be going somewhere that day, even if it was with Mr Boggle. I had never been to a museum before.

I remember that Mr Boggle told everyone, 'Do not touch things,' which was a shame. A sign in every room said it, too. 'DO NOT TOUCH!' Over and over, in every room.

Now, Mr Boggle can't see very well, so it was a mystery how it happened but somehow, I got separated from him and my class. I searched for them in vain. It was no use, alas – they had disappeared, maybe forever.

As I sat planning for my survival, an interesting thing happened – I was cast under a spell. Not a goblin's work I am sure, or an elf's, but a spell nonetheless. I could tell, because I felt a little bit different.

As if in a trance, I was led away. Along corridors, around corners, up lifts and down I went. I was on a tour, minus Mr Boggle and my dear classmates, who I was missing terribly – well, maybe not at all, now that I think back on it.

Mr Boggle or no Mr Boggle, no nook or cranny would escape my eager gaze.

I quite enjoyed my tour.

I searched for Mr Boggle without success.

But the thrill of meeting so many people of the past soon made me forget school and other such dreary things.

↑ I saw a creature of
exquisite beauty ↗

For now I was mixing with empresses and queens. 'Hello,' I said to each and every one of them. 'My name is Horrible Harriet – who are you?' There wasn't too much time for a chat, alas.

I learnt nothing from this woman →

I imagined how it might be to be royal, and have a statue made of me for people to admire.

She was close to to being my favourite royal so far.

44

I couldn't quite put my finger on why, but with all these royals I felt so at home.

I was almost hypnotised by the gaze of mystery

DONT TOUCH!

I saw a beautiful chair. But who had time to stop?

How nice it would be having servants to help around the house. Because I am an excellent cook, they'd only be used for cleaning up, and maybe trying out my exciting and adventurous recipes, which are world famous.

On I went, moved by the mysterious power, all the time asking questions and taking notes in my head. 'What's it like being Queen?' I asked, and received all the answers anyone could want.

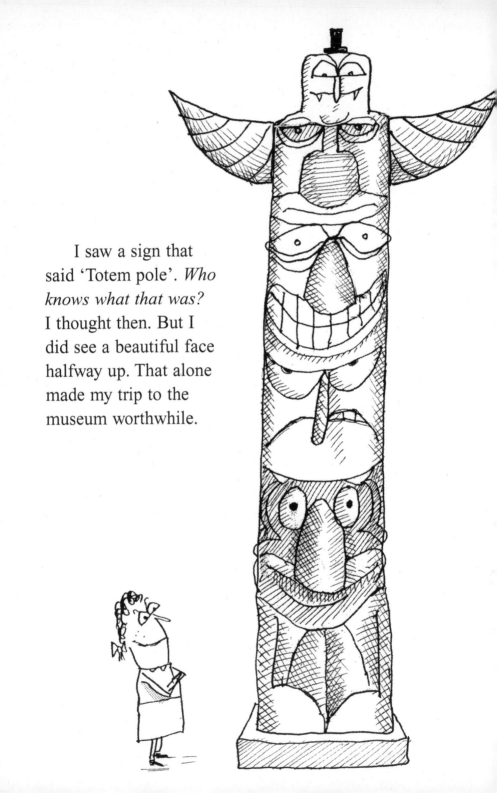

I saw a sign that said 'Totem pole'. *Who knows what that was?* I thought then. But I did see a beautiful face halfway up. That alone made my trip to the museum worthwhile.

I saw a hat that would be a perfect fit →

I talked to all the people. There wasn't much time to stop – I was busy. There was a lot to see.

The spell of the old things was strong at this stage.

49

'Ancient Roman coins,' said a sign.
How nice, I thought, to have
your head on some money.

NAUGHTY IV IN EXTREMUS

All this stuff inside glass cases –
about as interesting as old shoelaces.
I thought that way initially
till I found things that
looked like ME.

From the distance, I heard
a voice. 'Harriet! Harriet! Where
are you? We have a bus to catch,'
cried the voice of Mr Boggle. I tried
and tried to answer his call but
could not, for I was silenced by the
mysterious power of the museum.
But luckily for me I found a comfy
spot to sit and wait.

Anyone else would have given up, but not H.H.

After that trip to the museum I was never the same. I had a lot to think about.

But Reader, was this the proof I needed to fill in my family tree??

I didn't know it then but the proof I needed had been before my eyes and soon would be under my nose. →

54

Chapter 4

AN UNEXPECTED ARRIVAL

Early the next day, I was in for another big surprise. There was a *Bang! Bang! Bang!* on the front door. I thought it might be Sir Fred with another letter, so I raced downstairs to investigate. But there was no Sir Fred. And no letter. Just a big old chest on the path.

I looked but there was no one in sight.

I took the chest upstairs. On the lid it had the letters H.R.H.H.H.

↑ This means 'Her Royal Highness Horrible Harriet'.

I couldn't wait to open it. Who knew what scary creature lurked inside, ready to jump out and grip my throat with its icy claws? I bravely brushed away cobwebs and spiders, then shone my torch deep down into the dusty darkness. 'Hello!' I said. 'Is anyone in there?'

57

I delved deeply into the dark depths.

It turned out that the chest was full of treasures. There were photos galore of people in fancy dress. Lucky for me, someone (hundreds of years ago) had written on the backs of the photos everything I needed to know about the faces on the front. And because I was a history expert (almost a professor), I could fill in any information gaps myself anyway.

my housework
would have to wait.

HRH HORRIBLE HARRIET

I had a feeling that the chest and the treasures
inside it held the answers to my problem.

Chapter 5

LONG-LOST RELATIVES

Into the eyes of ancient beauties I gazed.

As usual I was right. Slowly and carefully, from the deep darkness, I took out photos that had been hidden from the light for hundreds of years. I gasped when I looked on the back of the first photo I found. And I ask you, who could not but gasp – for it was of Queen Harrietabanana, Ancient Egyptian Empress, daughter of the legendary Cleoparriot. She was holding a fine photo of her husband, the Pharaoh.

Though the photo of her was fairly faded, only
a fool could fail to see how alike she and I were.
We were both beautiful. (Me a bit more than her.)
Written on the back in ancient hieroglyphics (which
I am an expert in understanding) it said that her
mother was Harrietanoonoo the Third, the beloved
mother of Harrietutabooboo the First, second cousin of
Harrietabanana's half-brother boy-king, Hulubalooloo,
who crossed the desert three thousand years ago on an
elephant.

I took careful notes and added each name to my family tree straight away, for it was obvious that these were my ancient cousins. How much proof did Sir Huckleberry Rucksack want? Who cares! I'm the boss.

I worked out this was a relative of the ancient Egyptian empress I had seen in the museum. Just before I saw those Roman coins...remember? You'd better – there'll be a test at the end.

Filling in my family tree was going to be easier than I'd thought.

The next treasure was a signed photo of marvellous monarch Harrizabethe the Fourth. That smile! We could have been twins. A tear came to my eye. And those eyes – the sort that follow you when you look in a mirror...

On the back it said she was the cousin of the daughter of the mother of the ninth wife of Henry the Eighth's sister's best friend. And a *very* close friend of Elizabeth the First (Queen of England)...not her, but her ironing lady's mother. Look, I'm only telling you some things here. I can't be bothered going over everything.

Regards
Harrizabethe

Another fantastic find was a framed photo of
the famous Queen Horribilius the First, Empress of the
ancient kingdom of Horrietania, clutching her royal orb.
I could tell we were related, as she looked really regal.
And indeed we were, for notes in her very own
handwriting on the back said that her great-aunt was
related to the son of Harrietanoonoo's daughter
Noonoribilis. I found a branch for *her* straight away.
The tree was filling up fast.

↑ This is an orb... look it up

↗ This could have been me!

One of my favourite relatives I found after wiping away the dust of centuries was ferocious warrior Queen Numee Poowah. She was aboard her flaming chariot. According to the notes on the back, she was heading to a battle. (Well, she wouldn't be going shopping, would she, I ask you. She would have servants or slaves for that.) Mr Boggle had mentioned her in history lessons, but I'd never known she was a relative of mine.

68

Next, spookily, some ancient Roman coins with labels attached fell from an envelope. No wonder the spell had led me to the Roman coin department at the museum – all those empresses on the coins were my ancient Roman family!

In the same envelope was a signed photo of another Roman, Empress Naughty in Extremus. She was having lunch.

I was thrilled to be learning so much about history. My history.

Then I found myself staring
into the eyes of a rare beauty,
Scary Marie Hantwarnette.
Her mother's best friend
worked for the Empress
of Austria's sister, and she
was always playing dress-ups.
What a delight *she* must have been.
That sweet face, the eyes, the mouth.
She and I could've been sisters.

There were loads
more things but
there's not the
space here for
every detail.

This is Elise,
the Empress of
Austria's Sister

By the way this photo of me is here by mistake. It's me in another musical. →

This is Scary Marie ↑

Dear Reader, just when I thought I'd had every surprise possible, I found a photo worn by time and chewed by rats.

On the back, in ancient Norwegian, which by the way I am an expert speaker of, it said 'Victorious Valerie the Viking Invader'. It showed her ready for action.

Had Valerie the Viking led me to the helmet in the museum that day? Had she been trying to reach me from times long past?

*In days long gone,
a Horrible Harriet
may have moved around
in a golden chariot.*

Valerie the Viking – Victorious. ↑

Dracularriet, about to strike.

Mr Boggle had told us in class that lots of families have their black sheep. And, wouldn't you know it, I soon found mine… On the back of this photograph it said: 'Whoever looketh at this here photographe, do knoweth that it was taken in thy year 1702 in ye kingdom of Transylvania West. Thee beauty whom your eyes gazeth at is ye ruler of this here kingdom. Her nameth is… Empress Dracularriet. Signed in secret by her secretary and slave, Elsie.'

Dracularriet out for a midday stroll

Well. I can hardly tell you what a thrill *that* was.

I found another black sheep – Harey Mary, one-eyed pirate princess, scourge of the seven seas. She was born to royal blood but preferred to live a life of badness aboard her boat *The Horror*. Related by birth to Empress Dracularriet (second cousin), she was a member of the Royal House of Numee Poowah via her father King Bong Bong's stepmother, the Queen of Phalompia.

Now where was I? Oh yes. Queens, princesses, empresses, rulers, ancient invaders, all of them my dear, dear relatives. You must just believe everything I say, Reader, or else. I wrote all their names down. My pencil had been blunt twenty-four times since I'd begun. Ancient photo after ancient photo, coin after coin – even some paintings, maps and books…they all showed the same thing. That I was linked right back through history to these beauties of royal blood.

With great patience I was filling in the gaps.

I stood back and proudly admired my handiwork. I would send Sir Phinias Flashbank the finished family tree as soon as possible. It didn't surprise me that I came from a long, long list of bold and scary types, afraid of nothing.

Chapter 6

I PREPARE TO DEPART

I've a list of things — for the teachers — to buy as I'm going to bake them a tasty pie.

I was ready to meet my destiny. But even though it was the school holidays, I had my after-school chores to do. For instance, the teachers in the cellar needed to be fed. And they had to do my holiday homework. So I decided to cook them a pie to keep them happy. I spared no effort to get the best-quality ingredients.

Here is the recipe, which I don't mind sharing now
that you are members of the H. HARRIET FAN CLUB. You
may like to try it on your friends.

My pie pastry's a miracle, ever so nice.
The secret, I tell you, is essence of mice.
For instructions now listen, learn and take note.
As a cook I'm quite brilliant. Don't mind if I gloat.
First stir up a bowl of warm frog's legs and lizards.
Then mix in a pile of stale grasshopper gizzards.
Add pig's breath, two bat wings and bugs – about five.
Already the pie-mix will look…quite alive.
Prod a few spiders into the pot.
Then stir very carefully, until all is hot.
Pour into the pie case. Don't stand back and gape.
Push down on the lid or the mix might escape.
Oops, I forgot now, add one monster's eye…
then into the oven put this wonderful pie.
I'm sure you will like it.
Mr Scruffy and Miss Plume do.
I've heard no complaints,
at least not from those two.

Horrible Harriet

by H. Harriet ~~poet~~ poet

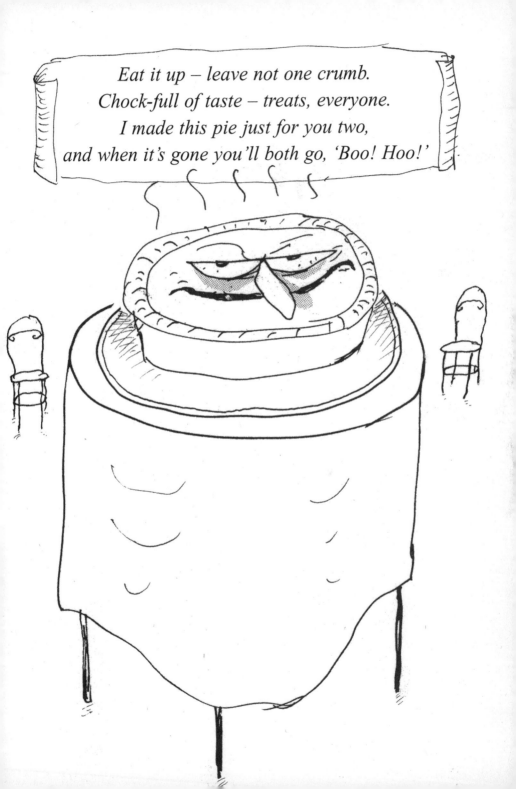

As well as a week's supply of my pie, I threw Miss Plume a bone. She was thrilled with her treat. 'Excellent for the teeth,' she said with a snarl.

Mr Scruffy began to sulk, so he got a treat, too. He wasn't happy at all that I was leaving.

From The Cellar

~~Tuesday~~
Thursday.

Dear Your Royal Highness

Just a note to thank you
for the ~~lovely~~ delicious pie, you are so
~~kind~~ thoughtful and, such a
good cook. We are both
very happy in the cellar.
Thanks for the nice new
doormats and curtains too.
FROM your ~~great~~ grateful
teachers.

Miss Patsy Plume
       and MR Cedric Scruffy

⟵ PS. THANK YOU FOR the TREATS

↑ See this note from the teachers.
It's a coincidence that their
writing looks just like mine.

85

Even my plants were snappy.
No one wanted me to go. ↓

Mr Chicken had permission to stay while I was away, but I made sure the fridge was double-locked. To be on the safe side, before I packed I also warned Mr Scruffy and Miss Plume to hide their treats and any leftover pie under their beds.

Now that my chores were done, I was free to leave
for the railway station to begin my journey of a lifetime.
At last I was going to visit my stately home and claim
my inheritance.

Chapter 7

MY THRILLING JOURNEY

As the train left the station I practised making people feel relaxed and at their ease. This is what I read someone who is royal is supposed to do. Anyway, this would be the last time I went anywhere with the common people. Next time I'd be aboard my own *royal* train. There'd be a royal cook, a butler, a lady-in-waiting (whatever that means...I must look it up), a wardrobe helper, ironing lady, hairdressers and probably an orchestra.

And whenever I arrived somewhere…ANYWHERE… I knew everyone would want to have their photo taken with me. Who could blame them? There would be people lined up needing to be knighted. Oh, what a nuisance. But I was sure there would be many thrilling royal duties that I would enjoy as well, which others would enjoy seeing me do.

Certainly there would *always* be people wanting an autograph. I'd already planned for this. I had a stamp to carry with me everywhere. It had 'H.R.H. Miss HORRIBLE HARRIET' on it.

For now, though, I didn't mind sharing a seat with some ordinary people. It was my way of saying goodbye to my old life. Soon I would be having a new, royal one. I thought about what wonders lay before me.

Of course, for my coronation I would need a crown. I could borrow that from the museum. They wouldn't mind, and even if they did, I'd be the Queen so I would issue a Royal Command.

Here I am, looking like a queen already →

And I would have to get used to subjects kissing my royal hand, I supposed. If they refused, there would be BIG trouble. And anyone who dared BITE the royal hand – I'd have them locked up straight away.

My trip in the royal coach for my coronation would be spectacular, with millions of my fans (including those from school) lined up outside waiting to catch a glimpse of the royal smile and the royal wave.

Readers, note my perfect royal wave.

↳ Me, more magnificent than ever.

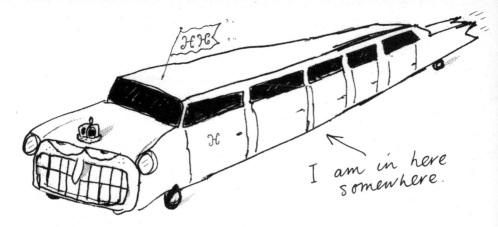

I am in here somewhere.

There'd be the official photos of me with my crown and cloak and orb.

As soon as I had the time, I would visit my old school in the Royal Harrietmobile. I would not necessarily get big-headed just because I was their Empress. I might boss them about *a bit* more than usual, but then, how exciting for my class to have me call and pose for a photograph with them and Mr Boggle in all my royal finery.

PROCLAMATION.

Monday

The 👑 Palace

Her maJesty wisHes it to be known that she SHall be visiting the school tomorRow morning for a tour and inspectiOn and she expects very special treatment like cʊrtsying and bowing. Plus there must be a MOrning tEa and herE is what I want, Cakes lemonade aɴnd party pies followed by a speCial treat. She shall be visiting her old place IN The Tower so it'd

better BE neat. See yoU At 9.ocl0CK.

\ Bye For NOW. *Queen Harriet* x

Though I would
probably leave my
orb at the palace,
as it's heavy, I think.

Just because I'm
Queen, it won't stop
me having fun. →

WELCOME BACK
YOUR MAJESTY!

Reader, can you spot me?

Naturally I would wear my crown always – well, most times anyway.

When Queen, I would put my subjects at their ease by reading one of my poems.

I'd ask them if they liked it, then look at them straight in the eye and ask if they were telling the truth. I am already an expert hypnotist, and I know from experience that this skill would be handy in difficult royal situations.

The Look which commands attention

Then I would go on a royal tour of the playground where I used to relax with the common people before I was Queen. I might call on some special friends to discuss old times and carry my train.

In every schoolroom there would be a painting of me at the front, high up so no one could graffiti it.

Everyone wants to carry the royal train.

Of course there would be lots of souvenirs of me for people to collect. I would be loved. And in all corners of the land, people would have signed pictures of me, which they would understandably cherish.

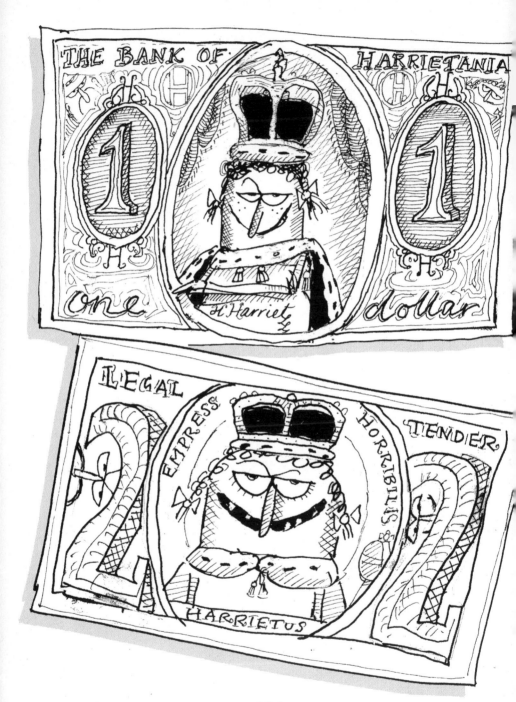

And what a thrill for people to open their purse or wallet and see my face inside. I could have as much money as I liked, because my picture would be on every coin and banknote. Which means that I would own all of it. Maybe.

105

With so many official duties and public appearances opening buildings and smashing bottles against the sides of ships for good luck every day, I might get tired of being adored. Some days I'd need to just feel normal, and would sneak away from the palace to visit the shops, incognito, for some chips.

And sometimes I might slip in to the cinema unnoticed after the lights had gone down and see a movie. I wouldn't catch a bus, because people would see me – I'd have the Coronation Coach wait for me round the corner.

My head would be everywhere and on everything. What a thrill for everyone, especially me. I would be licked on stamps, of course, and then put in post boxes.

And there would be statues of me in parks for the pleasure of the population. I would make a beautiful statue, there is no doubt in my mind.

'Destination in five minutes!' I heard a voice call.

The 'many moods of the monarch' stamp series.

Licking my own face →

HORRIBILIS
HARRIETUS
MAGNIFICO
REGINA

It was time for me to look my best.

A band was probably practising for my arrival right at this minute. And school children would be waiting to bow to me, with their bouquets of flowers ready to hand over. So I thought that I had better freshen up in the train bathroom.

Mirror, mirror, on the wall,
I can't resist it when you call.
No one cares what's your opinion,
for looks like mine are one in a million.

I couldn't wait to move in to my stately home.
I would make myself comfy, then make a speech of
greetings to my servants. I would say that if they did
their job well, I would cook a treat for them every now
and then. Maybe that pie I told you about.

When the train arrived at the station I looked for the crowd, but there wasn't one. The Lord Mayor was nowhere to be seen (I'd imagined he'd say more than a few words of welcome). What's more, I couldn't hear a band playing.

'They must have got the day wrong,' I explained to a lady at the tourist information office. She was not much help when I asked where I might find my royal coach.

'I am looking for my stately home as well,' I told her. 'Do you know who I am?'

It had been a big journey and I was looking forward to a banquet. I was in no mood for waiting, so I set off.

Chapter 8

INHERITANCE AT LAST

It was a long walk, and I don't mind telling you I was feeling grumpy. But as soon as a stately home appeared in the distance my bad mood mysteriously lifted.

I was looking forward to the rejoicing that would soon take place when my servants welcomed me to my new house.

I unlocked the front gate and walked up a gravel path. My stately home looked quite nice, and I remember thinking that I could rule from here after my coronation. Guards at the gate would keep autograph pests away. That is, until I had done my royal duties.

Anyway, back to my arrival at H.H. House. Now, Reader, I hope you are concentrating, for this was a journey of a lifetime, and as I said once before, it won't happen to you because, sad and unfair though it may seem, you are not like me. Even if you wish you were. And many do. Forget it. I will tell you much in this book, but there is a lot that shall stay a secret forever.

Boldly I strode up the big Stone steps,
three at a time.

I seized the mighty doorknocker, and with a *Boom! Boom! Boom!* I announced my arrival.

'Horrible Harriet is here!' I called, summoning the servants. The door swung open with a loud creak and groan. There was no answer. Maybe the servants were having afternoon tea. Bravely I walked in. I say 'bravely' because there could have been a zombie waiting for me behind the door.

At first I felt at home in my new house. It was
very big, and I remember thinking that I hoped pushy
Mr Chicken wouldn't want to move in and take over
and expect to be knighted.

120

I wasn't missing him at all. There was no one about, but I didn't feel alone.

BUT before I had time to get comfortable
something strange began to happen, and for a moment
I remembered the museum. It was happening again.

As much as I tried, I could not resist this
mysterious power of old things. It told me to forget my
suitcase and follow it. 'Straight away,' it ordered. I did
as I was told and followed.

Even though I was in a deep trance, I noticed when I passed a mirror that I didn't look any different.

Off I went – taken for a tour around my stately home. I hoped we would go to a kitchen soon, as I was hungry and felt like a sandwich, at least.

I saw many beautiful things.

And I felt something was seeing me.

I said hello as I marched past women in
fancy dresses.

'Welcome home, Harriet,' they whispered.

'Thank you,' I answered. 'Nice to meet you.'

127

Yes, well, that was all very friendly but it was getting late. In fact, it was around the time when Mr Chicken and I usually went for a walk. By now I knew he had probably discovered the spare fridge key. And eaten everything inside.

At last I found a place to sleep, thanks to expert
directions from the spell. It wasn't as comfy as my nest
back at home, but I was tired and fell straight to sleep.
I dreamt about all the royal relatives from long ago I
had now got to know. In the morning when I woke up
I wondered if the spell had worn off.

I wondered if the spell had worn off.

But alas,
the spell was more
powerful than ever.

What is this place?
I wondered as I wandered.
*And how did I come to have
so many ancestors?*

I passed a painting that looked
a lot like Queen Numee Powah.
Was I related to *everyone* royal?

So many questions, but as I said,
I'm not answering all of them here. I was
looking forward to breakfast. If
only the spell would show some
mercy and take me to where I
could have breakfast. What was
the use of a big stately home
if there was no food in a fridge?
Or worse still, no fridge at all!!

I had thought royal people
would have fridges
STUFFED with food.
Anyway.

131

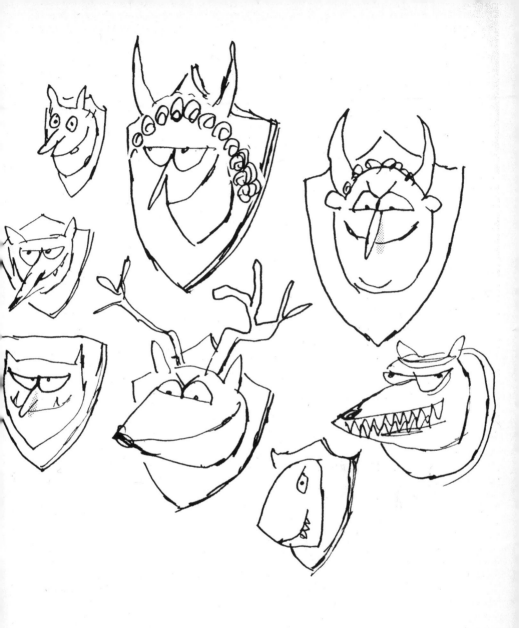

Even though I was in a trance, I could tell that I
was close to my ancestors.

On I went, along a
passage to a window…
where the spell let me
stop for a minute.

In the distance, I saw
a house. A little house.

I went straight out to investigate.

Breakfast at last

On the door it said 'H.R.H. Horrible Harriet' – Her Royal Highness Horrible Harriet.

Inside was breakfast, all ready, and a card that said 'Welcome'. There was a pot of tea and some scones on the table. And warm toast. Just what I needed.

136

It was hard work being royal. I ate my breakfast up and decided to relax.

What was the point of being royal if you couldn't relax?

137

I didn't know why, but suddenly I began to worry about Mr Scruffy and Miss Plume. They would need to be fed. And my friends back at school – how they would miss me. And my poetry! And I had left my diary at home. And of course there was You-Know-Who, but we won't mention his name.

I wondered whether
mr Chicken had eaten
the teachers' treats.

It was hard to decide whether to go or stay in my stately home, so I wrote a list.

MY LIST (PRIVATE) No looking!

Good reasons to STAY
- stately home is nice – And BIG!
- I could rule from here.
- I Am away from mR chicken (a PEST)

GOOD Reasons to GO Home
- My poetry and my diary left at home.
- my concertos. (remember my concertos)
- mR SCRUFFY + miss Plume need feeding
- fridge needs protecting from mr chicken.
- my midnight walks with mr c.
- school friends will miss me if I stay here.
ALSO MY cooking.... (if I am Queen someone else will do it and I dont want that)
as NO ONE CAN COOK LIKE mE!
signed, Horrible Harriet.

That solved everything.

140

Chapter 9

So, Reader, as you can see, here I am back at home, writing to you all about my wonderful travels. Not to mention my relatives – who you must feel like you know by now. And I suppose you are wondering why I came back?

Well, I decided to have
my coronation later.
So I got on the train
and I went back home.

And I'm glad that I did – for Mr Chicken HAD got into my fridge, just as I'd expected. And he HAD made himself quite at home. And Mr Scruffy and Miss Plume WERE running low on my pie and needed feeding. And school had started and homework was piling up.

'Fancy coming home to this mess!'

And friends
were missing me.

↑ On my return, everyone rushed to greet me.

And not only that, I wanted to tell everyone about my adventure – though I later changed my mind. *Let them buy the book!* I thought.

My trip gave me many recipe ideas, and between cooking, poetry, my diary, concerto-writing and school, I have not had much time to do anything else. How would I have fitted in being a monarch or even a duchess with all that, I ask you?!

Go on, admit it. No one can cook like me!

After my triumphant return, I wrote a letter to Sir Monsonby Crackerjack, or whatever his name was.

> Wed.
>
> Dear Sir Mon soon Black jack
>
> Thanks a LOT for your help. I have seen my stately home, which is nice, and met the RElatives. But ~~tell~~ tell the Royal family I will move into the Royal palace another time ~~free~~ because I have things to do at home. If it's ok with you I'll have my cORONation later.
>
> Bye for now.
> HRH ~~Horrible~~ Harriet

I haven't got a reply yet, but one will come, I'm sure. He's probably out to lunch.

Anyway. Now I have the best of both worlds – I have a holiday house on the coast to visit if I want to see my relatives...

…and a stately home of my own right here. Which you may visit. But only if you make a Royal Appointment first. And don't ask questions, for it is a long story.

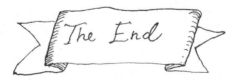

The End

The H. HARRIET FAN CLUB

PRESIDENT: H. HARRIET

Before you are a proper member you must answer the following questions.

By order of the President – which is me.

1. Who do you know the secrets of that is royal? (well, *some* of the secrets of)......................
2. Who has a friend that wears a top hat and is very big?...
3. Who lives in the top of the school tower?...
4. Who sleeps on a nest?...
5. Who is the best poet you know?...
6. Who is the best cook you know?.......................

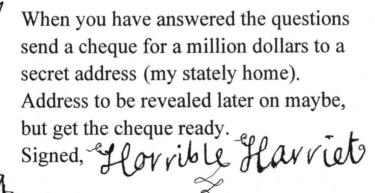

When you have answered the questions send a cheque for a million dollars to a secret address (my stately home). Address to be revealed later on maybe, but get the cheque ready.

Signed, *Horrible Harriet*

Books by my assistant,
Leigh
HOBBS.

About the Author

Mr Leigh Hobbs is an artist and an author. His work in painting, sculpture and animation has all primarily been about characters. This is especially so for the children's books he writes and illustrates, for which he is best known.

Horrible Harriet is but one of these creations. There is also Mr Chicken, Old Tom, Fiona the Pig and Mr Badger. And of course the Freaks in 4F, including Feral Beryl, Nearly Normal Nancy (she has three eyes) and Not So Nice Nora.

There is actually a world in which all of these misfits cohabit quite comfortably – and that world has been inside Mr Hobbs' head since childhood.